For my family, a few words cannot express my gratitude and love.
So, here is an entire book. You are my everything. —B.Z.

Copyright © 2018 by Bridgette Zou

Publisher's Cataloging-in-Publication Data

Names: Zou, Bridgette, author, illustrator.
Title: Norman and the nom nom factory / by Bridgette Zou.
Description: New York, NY: StarBerry Books, an imprint of Kane Press, Inc., 2018.
Identifiers: ISBN 9781635920321 (Hardcover) | 9781635920338 (ebook) | LCCN 2017953349
Summary: Norman the alien learns how to enjoy new foods and new discoveries when a strange visitor crash lands on Planet Gerp.
Subjects: LCSH Extraterrestrial beings--Juvenile fiction. | Food--Juvenile fiction. | Science fiction. | BISAC JUVENILE FICTION / Social Themes / New Experience | JUVENILE FICTION / Cooking & Food
Classification: LCC PZ7.Z7768 No 2018 | DDC [E]--dc23

Library of Congress Control Number: 2017953349

10 9 8 7 6 5 4 3 2 1

First published in the United States of America in 2018 by StarBerry Books, an imprint of Kane Press, Inc.
Printed in China

StarBerry Books is a trademark of Kane Press, Inc.

Book Design: Michelle Martinez

Visit us online at www.kanepress.com

 Like us on Facebook
facebook.com/kanepress

 Follow us on Twitter
@KanePress

This is Norman.

And this is his Nom Nom factory.

Norman and his factory are on

Planet Gerp.

It is very, very
FAR AWAY
from anything else.

Just the way Norman likes it. Nice and quiet.

Every day Norman works in his Nom Nom factory making his galaxy-famous Nom Noms.

And every day he uses the exact same super secret Nom Nom recipe invented by his beloved Grandma Nancy.

Even when Norman was just a little fluffball, he would help Grandma Nancy make Nom Noms.

She would always say,

"Norman, guard this recipe!

Don't show it to anyone and don't change it.

It's top secret."

Everyone in the galaxy loves
Nom Noms. Including Norman.
Norman eats *only* Nom Noms.

A bowl of Nom Noms for breakfast,

a plate of Nom Noms for lunch,

a tray of Nom Noms for dinner.

Norman loves Nom Noms, just the way they are.

It was a very normal, very quiet day at the Nom Nom factory when suddenly—

Rushing outside, Norman saw it. . . .

A SPACESHIP!

The ship popped open and out climbed a creature Norman had never seen before.

"Greetings, galactic friend! I'm Chip. My ship seems to be having some problems."

"Clearly," said Norman.

"What's your name?" asked Chip.

"Norman."

"Can I call you Normie?"

"No."

"Manny?"

"No. Me, Norman. You, Chip."

"What is this place? Seems a little . . . empty," said Chip.

"This is *my* planet, Gerp! And this is *my* factory. Just me, my factory, and my Gerp. No need for any Chips, and certainly no need for any spaceships!"

"I'm sorry, fellow galaxy dweller, but I'll need a few days to fix my ship," Chip replied. "Looks like you've got plenty of room here. Perhaps I could . . ."

GERP
POPULATION:
1
(NORMAN)

CLICK!

SNAP!

"Stay?!" cried Norman.

Norman loved being alone on Gerp, but he also couldn't forget what his grandma had always taught him: one, guard the top secret Nom Nom recipe, and two, practice good manners. Chip was invited to stay for dinner.

As they sat down at the table, Norman asked Chip, "So, do you like Nom Noms?" "What's a Nom Nom?" replied Chip. Norman gasped.

"This is a Nom Nom."

He sighed lovingly. "It's the most delicious thing in the entire galaxy. No, the entire universe! That's why it's the only thing I eat. I've never bothered to try anything else," declared Norman. "Here, have some!" Chip couldn't believe his ears. "Only Nom Noms?! So you've never tried Starm? Or Slizzah? Not even Bick Bork? If I try a Nom Nom, will you try a Starm?" Chip chirped.

"No."

"How about a nibble of Bing? Just a taste? It would be rude if I didn't offer you something! Try it. You might love it, you never know."

But Norman refused.

"No, no, no!" he shouted. "I won't like it!"

"But if you don't try it, how will you know you don't like it?" Chip replied.

"Well . . . I'm not sure. No one's ever asked me to try something new before."

Norman was stumped.

Chip didn't ask again. He took a
Nom Nom from the bowl and popped
it into his mouth.

"Wow, tasty," he said.

"Thanks," said Norman. "I made
them myself."

That night after dinner, Norman
couldn't stop thinking about what Chip
had said. He had never tried anything new
before. That sounded scary.

The next day, Norman kept thinking about Chip's challenge to try something new.

He thought about it while preparing breakfast,

while concocting the Nom Noms' secret recipe,

while sipping on afternoon tea,

while packing up a shipment of Nom Noms,

and even while counting the planets and stars

after a long day of work at the Nom Nom factory.

At dinner, Norman shyly asked Chip his important question.

"Do you like everything you try?"

"Not always," replied Chip. "But trying new things is how I make my best discoveries! I was supposed to turn left at planet Earth, but I didn't. And that's how I ended up on Gerp and discovering Nom Noms . . . and meeting you!"

Then Chip frowned. "But . . . once I turned right at Mars and ended up in a swamp."

BIG SWAMP

WRONG WAY

"You're quite adventurous for being so little," said Norman.

"Well . . . sometimes it's the littlest things that lead to the biggest adventures." Chip smiled.

"I've never tried anything new. . . . I wouldn't even know where to start," whispered Norman.

"What about some Bing?" offered Chip. "We can try it together!"

"What does it taste like?" asked Norman.

"I'm not sure! I picked it up right before I landed—er, crashed—into Gerp," said Chip.

"You promise you'll try some, too?" said Norman.

"Promise," replied Chip.

He sniffed.

Norman poked.

And finally took a taste.

SNIFF
SNIFF

After what seemed like an eternity, Norman spoke.
"Well, it doesn't taste like Nom Noms," he declared.
"Well, that's because it's Bing," said Chip. "Have some more!"
"Nope, that's enough adventure for one day."

Chip trailed Norman into the Nom Nom factory.

"Ahem, Norman, I'm going to leave you some more Bing . . . right here . . . just in case you change your mind."

"Don't worry, I won't. I've decided that Nom Noms are the only thing for me."

Norman went on about his factory business making the Nom Nom recipe.

He added a little of this . . . a little of that . . .

Norman didn't notice what his paw was reaching for until . . .

A new ingredient?! The ultimate disgrace!
Norman had ruined the top secret recipe.
Grandma Nancy would never forgive him.
As Norman's panic grew, he suddenly saw
Chip reaching for one of the disastrous creations.

"DON'T!"
Norman yelled.

But it was too late.

"Oh my Gerp! I've poisoned
Chip!" Norman bawled.

"*Oh my Gerp* is right!" said Chip. "Try this! Please, Norman. You MUST try it!"
"You're alive!" Norman shouted.
"Obviously. Now try!"

"But . . . what if . . ." Norman hesitated.

"What if? What if you like it . . . ?" asked Chip.

Norman's fur prickled, his paws began to sweat, and his stomach felt
as if it were filled with comets. But finally, he leaned in for a taste. . . .

"Oh. My. **GERP!**" exclaimed Norman, "These are incredible. No. They're . . . they're delicious! What should I do with them? What is this feeling? I've never felt it before!"

"I think it's called making a discovery. Nifty, huh?" chirped Chip. A grin started to spread on Norman's face. "A *discovery*. Wow."

Walking out of the factory that evening, Norman looked up at the stars. Turning to his new friend Chip, he asked, "So, what else do you think is out there? You know . . . to discover and try."

Chip smiled and replied, "I don't know, but I think we can find out."